Between Us and Abuela

A Family Story from the Border

Mitali Perkins

ILLUSTRATIONS BY Sara Palacios

Farrar Straus Giroux
New York

For Madhusree —M. P.
To my parents. And those who have left a country
and family behind in pursuit of a new path. —S. P.

Abuela stars in all of Mamá's stories, but my only memory is a voice calling me "angelita." We haven't seen my grandmother in five years. But today is La Posada Sin Fronteras, and we are taking a bus to the border to meet her.

We take the bus to Border Field State Park in San Diego. Mamá's needles are clicking away. We're knitting a scarf for Abuela to wear on the long journey back to her village. I did most of it myself, but Mamá is finishing it.

Juan has a present for Abuela, too. Most of the big piece of cardboard is blank. But in the middle are Mary and Joseph, two short sticks with arms. "Las Posadas" are small squares labeled: "Inns. No rume."

When the bus drops us off, we walk and walk along the beach. Juan carries his picture high so it doesn't get sandy or wet.

We see the top of a white lighthouse. Mamá's hand tightens on mine. "That's in Mexico," she says.

We walk closer. Two high, strong fences stretch along the border, reaching deep into the sea.

Border patrol officers are waiting. "Twenty-five people at a time," the shorter one tells us. "Each group gets thirty minutes."

We stand in line. Visitors press against the second fence, singing and laughing with friends and family in Mexico.

But the fence only has tight, small openings. We might be able to squeeze our gift through to Abuela, but what about Juan's picture? It will never fit.

Mamá drapes the scarf around my neck. "Maybe when he sees her, he'll forget it," she whispers.

We wait while another group goes in. A gusty wind makes the palm trees dance. They lean to the Mexico side, away from us.

Finally, it's our turn. The gate swings open. Is Abuela there?

"¡Sylvia! ¡Sylvia!"

I know that voice! That's Mamá's name!

A pinkie wiggles through the fence. "¡Juan! ¡María! ¡Estoy aquí!"

"Abuela! Abuela!"

"¡Guapito!" She calls Juan her little handsome. "¡María, angelita!"

I am still her angel!

Mamá's words trip over Abuela's. Cousins, chickens, corn—
everything in the village has grown. Abuela drops kisses on our
fingers. She is short, brown, plump, and jolly. Hugging her
would feel like hugging a chunk of cookie dough.

Juan's eye is pressed against a hole. One edge
of the picture is in the dirt. Maybe Mamá was
right. He has forgotten it, at least for now.

The minutes race by. A priest reads the Christmas
story. He leads a carol about Las Posadas. I close my
eyes to hear Abuela and Mamá sing. For a moment,
the fences are invisible.

The officer opens the gate. "Time's up."

Suddenly, I remember the scarf—Abuela's gift! I try to push the end of it through the mesh.

Abuela's pinkie touches the soft wool. "¿Para mí? ¡Gracias, María!"

The officer strides over and grabs the scarf. His fingers squeeze and clutch the wool.

It's taken so long to knit. Is he going to keep it? But he hands it back to Mamá.

"Sorry," he says. "We can't let anything through the fence."

She drapes it back around my neck. "We'll send it by mail, María."

But now Abuela can't wear it on the long journey home.

The gate bangs shut. We're outside.

Juan holds up his picture. "What about *my* gift?"

"Sorry, Papi," Mamá says. "No way to get it across."

Juan's tears become a howl. Abuela calls out her worry: "¿Qué pasó?"

Mamá can't explain. Juan is too loud. She steers him to a bench.

There *has* to be a way to get that picture to Abuela. I glare at the fences.

Two seagulls take off from the sand and soar over the border.

Suddenly, I have an idea. "Mamá, give me your knitting bag!"

She looks up. "Why, María?"

"You'll see. Juan, I'll get your picture to Abuela."

He stops crying and hands it to me.

"¡Abuela, espérate!" I call to my grandmother. Will she hear?
Will she wait?

"¡Claro, María!" she shouts.

Everything I need is in Mamá's knitting bag. I start by trimming the cardboard into a diamond. My brother doesn't stop me. There's still plenty of space around Stick Mary and Stick Joseph. Next I lay two knitting needles, one longer, one shorter, across the corners, and fasten them in place with wool.

Mamá helps me attach one end of a ball of thin, strong yarn to the cross of needles. I poke a needle through the ball so two ends stick out.

"Better ask permission," Mamá says.

When I hold up my invention, the shorter officer shakes his head.
But the taller one takes it and looks at it closely. He smiles when he
sees Juan's drawing. "It won't be passing through the fence, right, kid?"

"No," I promise.

"The beach would be a better place," he says.

Mamá, Juan, and I head to the shore.

"Juan, throw the picture up when I shout. Mamá, be ready with
the scissors."

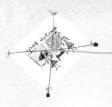

Juan lifts the picture. I take the string, turn my back, and run. "Throw, Juan!"

At first, the yarn pulls taut behind me. But then the wind dies. The picture nose-dives into the sand.

Juan runs to get it. I spin the string back around the needle.

We try again.

Watchers on both sides of the border are calling out advice.

The patrol officer's voice booms down: "Don't give up, kid!"

For the third time, Juan runs to get the
picture while I twist up the wool.
We get back in our places.
"Throw, Juan!"

I race across the beach. The yarn pulls taut like it did
before. I glance over my shoulder. This time the ball unwinds
steadily, taking Abuela's gift up and up.

Juan's face is tipped back. "Go, go, go!" he screams.

Others join in and it becomes a chant. Everyone cheers when the picture rises as high as the fence.

"Mamá, the scissors!"

With one snip, she cuts the yarn. The wind holds, and Juan's gift soars over both fences, straight into Mexico.

Shouts come from our side.

"Where is it?"

"Keep an eye on it!"

Mexico answers.

"It's landed! It's in the sand!"

"Your grandmother has it!"

The crowd cheers. Juan does a victory dance.

We can't see through the fences, but I picture Abuela scurrying across the beach. She will pick up Juan's gift. She might even kiss Stick Mary and Stick Joseph. Then she will carry them as carefully as my brother did, all the way home.

AUTHOR'S NOTE

Las Posadas is a nine-day festival celebrated throughout Mexico and in other countries from December 16 until December 24. It is a time to remember the birth of Jesús and how his parents, María and José, searched for shelter on the night he was born. Turned away from the inns of Bethlehem, María gave birth to her baby and laid him in a manger instead.

Every night during Las Posadas, two people dress up as María and José. A procession of neighbors holding candles and poinsettias join them to knock on the door of an "inn" or "posada." On these nights, though, unlike that long-ago night in Bethlehem, this Holy Family and their companions are welcomed, sheltered, and feasted by their hosts.

La Posada Sin Fronteras ("The Inn Without Borders") is celebrated on one day during Las Posadas along the border between Mexico and the United States of America. People in Tijuana work with people in San Diego to plan the event. Friends and families gather in Friendship Park in San Diego and in Playas de Tijuana by the lighthouse in Tijuana. They sing traditional Posada carols, hear the stories of migrants living in the United States and in Mexico, and listen in silence to the naming of people who died trying to cross the border. Participants from many church traditions worship on both sides of the border with the primary border wall between them. On the US side, they stand in the area known as the enforcement zone, between the primary and secondary border walls, under the surveillance of Border Patrol officials.

Rules, fences, and walls along the border are in flux. This story is a fictional portrayal of the celebrations of La Posada Sin Fronteras that have taken place since 1993. In that walled setting, during one of those many events, I imagined one family separated by the border trying to share the joy of Christmas.

I am grateful to Pedro Rios, director of the American Friends Service Committee's U.S.-Mexico Border Program, for his guidance. If you are interested in supporting La Posada Sin Fronteras or participating in the event, you may find out more at afsc.org/office/san-diego-ca. Thanks also to my agent, Laura Rennert, the marvelous team at FSG/Macmillan, including my editor, Grace Kendall, and to Sara Palacios for her partnership in creating this story.

Farrar Straus Giroux Books for Young Readers
An imprint of Macmillan Publishing Group, LLC
120 Broadway, New York, NY 10271

Color separations by Bright Arts (H.K.) Ltd.
Printed in China by Toppan Leefung Printing Ltd., Dongguan City, Guangdong Province
Designed by Monique Sterling
First edition, 2019

1 3 5 7 9 10 8 6 4 2

mackids.com

Library of Congress Cataloging-in-Publication Data

Names: Perkins, Mitali, author. | Palacios, Sara, illustrator.
Title: Between us and Abuela / Mitali Perkins ; illustrations by Sara
    Palacios.
Description: [New York : Farrar Straus Giroux, 2019] | Summary: When María,
    Juan, and their mother go to the border between California and Mexico to
    visit their grandmother at Christmas, María must devise a way to get
    Juan's gift over the fence.
Identifiers: LCCN 2018036019 | ISBN 9780374303730 (hardcover)
Subjects: | CYAC: Gifts—Fiction. | Grandmothers—Fiction. | Brothers and
    sisters—Fiction. | Mexican Americans—Fiction. | Christmas—Fiction.
Classification: LCC PZ7.P4315 Bet 2019 | DDC [E] —dc23
LC record available at https://lccn.loc.gov/2018036019

Our books may be purchased in bulk for promotional, educational, or business use. Please contact your local bookseller or the Macmillan Corporate
and Premium Sales Department at (800) 221-7945 ext. 5442 or by email at MacmillanSpecialMarkets@macmillan.com.